SHAKY QUAKY JAKE

With thanks, I dedicate this book to family, friends, and caregivers who have supported me through all the shaking and quaking. -KDR

Dedicated to my kids, husband, and to all the hearts striving to be a better version today than they were yesterday. -JG

Developmental Editor: Leila Boukarim
Editorial Director: Janan Sarwar
Designer: Khizra Saeed

First Edition: 2024
ISBN: 9781957242095
Library of Congress Control Number: 2023935011

Visit us online at http://GlobalBookshelves.com

GLOBAL BOOKSHELVES
INTERNATIONAL, LLC

SHAKY QUAKY JAKE

Written by Kelly D. Roberts

Illustrated by Jveria Gauhar

I love library day at school.

I clutch the book I checked out.

"Are you cold?" the new librarian asks me as I sit down in the circle.

"No."

My face gets hot and I look down at my hands.

I wish the shaky quakies would stop.

When she asks for a book volunteer,
I drop my head and scrunch down.

Joey scootches away from me.

At lunch, I ask Rachel to carry my tray.

"Sure."
"Thanks!"

I try to open my milk.

After lunch, I struggle with the computer mouse.

The characters dance across the screen
and I hold in a snicker.

SWERVE! SWIVEL! SHAKE!

"What's so funny, Jake?"
Mr. Hernandez asks.

I place both hands on the
mouse to make it stay still.

"Gramma, can you hug my shaky quakies away?"
"Bad day, Jake?" she asks.

Playing video games helps me relax.
I try to hold the controller still.
But today, my thumb keeps jumping up
and down more than usual.

SHAKE! JUGGLE! JIGGLE! JUMP!

I drop the controller and punch the pillow beside me.

Gramma squeezes me.
"Let's make cookies!"

I try to drop the dough on the pan
but it plops off the spoon in a big gooey glop.

But Gramma doesn't care if the cookies
don't turn out perfectly round.

"Turn up the music, Jake. I love this song!"
I giggle as Gramma limps into a jig.

SHAKE   SASHAY   SHIMMY

We dance.

As the cookies bake, I set up the game board.

SHAKE! RATTLE! ROLL!

The pieces hit the floor when my hand bumps the board.

Gramma doesn't fuss. She just laughs and says,
"Let's set it up again, Jake."
I win two out of three games!

I grab Gramma's cane.
"We should stretch our legs. Let's go see the ducks."

We walk to the pond across the street
and we stand on the dock for a long time.

Gramma holds my hands until they are still
and calm like the water.

Gramma groans and shifts her legs.
"Are you okay, Gramma?"

"Oh, just these old bones complaining.
How do you feel?"

I don't respond right away.
After a while, I say, "Some days are hard."

She hugs me. "You are patient and kind. You're fun-loving and creative, too. Most of all, you try hard, and the best any of us can do is keep trying.

You know, Jake, everyone struggles with something. Some things are seen, some unseen. But you can't be embarrassed by the hard things. You're one of a kind!"

The next day, Ms. Schwisow, the art teacher, shares an announcement.

"Today, we will make lions to decorate the classroom for parent's night."

I start to turn red from the top of my head to the tip
of my toes as Rachel hands out the scissors.

My shaky quakies are back!

I can never hold the scissors.

Ms. Schwisow leans over and quietly says,
"Jake, I will come back to help you."

She turns away and walks to Joey, who has his hand up.

I look at the supplies in front of me.
Ms. Schwisow has been gone a long time.

SHAKE

TEAR

RIP!

I rip up the paper.

RIP

TEAR

SHAKE

I look down.

Carefully, I tear some more.

I get more paper.

Slowly but surely, the lion takes shape.

It does not look
like anyone else's.

I work hard and run out of glue.

Rachel shares hers.

I shake and quake and drop glue on my shirt.
I giggle and say, "I better not glue myself to the table!"

Ms. Schwisow puts her hand on my shoulder and says, "It's okay. It is washable glue, Jake."

Then she gasps. "Jake! Oh my!"

My heart beats hard in my chest, and I hold my breath.

I did not follow the directions.

I glance down at the scissors I had pushed away.

My face flushes.
My shaky quaky hands can barely hold the lion!

Then my friends come over to see my lion.

"Wish I thought of that!"

"Totally awesome!"

Back in the classroom, I boldly push my hand up when Mr. Hernandez asks for a book volunteer.

He nods at me.

"I brought my favorite book," I say.
"I need someone to hold it for me."

Joey raises his hand. "I want to do it."
I am going to tell the story I know by heart.

I look at my friends sitting in the circle.

Everyone is looking at me, which makes me shake
and quake more, but I don't care.

These are my classmates and my friends.
They don't mind that I shake and quake.

I can't wait to show Gramma my lion!

I tried my best, and all we can ever do is try.
Today is a good day.

RESPECTING OTHERS IN THE COMMUNITY

Respect means treating others kindly and fairly. Making respect a regular practice makes our world pleasant and communication more effective.
Author Kelly Roberts has come up with some simple ideas to help us be respectful.
How can YOU use these principles to guide your actions?

R **RECOGNIZE SIMILARITIES**
Consider your commonalities before thinking about differences when you meet a new classmate or teacher.

E **ENCOURAGE CURIOSITY**
Engage and smile! Curiosity is healthy, but be polite!

S **SUPPORT RESPECTFULLY**
Be considerate of how others would like to be treated.

P **PRACTICE EMPATHY**
Perform kindness in words and deeds. Regard everyone with courtesy.

E **EDUCATE YOURSELF**
If you have a question, ask direct questions. Save some for later if you have too many questions. Seek resources to learn more.

C **CONSIDER OPTIONS**
Decide the next step to take. Maybe you step in to help or just smile and give them space.

T **TRY AGAIN**
Mistakes happen when interacting with others. Forgive yourself and apply what you have learned.

Everyone has visible and hidden unique qualities, so be YOUnique.

GLOBAL BOOKSHELVES
INTERNATIONAL, LLC

A Note from the Author

Essential tremor (ET) is a neurological condition that causes a rhythmic trembling of the hands, head, voice, legs, or trunk. It is often confused with Parkinson's disease, although ET is more common and is not limited by age. According to the International Essential Tremor Foundation (IETF), as of 2023, ET affects an estimated 2% of the US population and millions more worldwide. Recent research shows that 20% of adults who have ET showed the symptoms at a young age. It is not fatal but worsens over time and significantly affects day-to-day living. Having been diagnosed in 2013 with this disorder, I understand only too well the frustration and isolation ET causes. Small motor activities like using a fork, brushing your teeth, and even writing are nearly impossible some days.

I wish to thank all the occupational and physical therapists who helped me cope with this disorder, and a special thank you to the IETF for encouraging me. The IETF is available as a contact for anyone wishing to know more. The more we talk about disabilities and accept every child as unique and complete as they are, the more we reduce the stigma and isolation disabled children feel. Education, kindness, and RESPECT are the keys to ending stigma and discrimination.

International Essential Tremor Foundation
PO Box 14005
Lenexa, Kansas 66285-4005
USA 888.387.3667 (toll free)
913.341.3880 (local)
EssentialTremor.org

ietf
International Essential Tremor Foundation
Your Voice for Essential Tremor

About the Author

Kelly D. Roberts lives in S.E. Washington state with her Shorkie puppy, Freyja. You can find them making new friends in the park, hanging out with Kelly's grandson, reading, or playing board games. Kelly homeschooled her children, then finished her degree in Early Childhood Education, spending time as a preschool teacher with the Early Childhood Education Assistance Program before retiring and pursuing a career in children's literature. She feels strongly that every child deserves to be loved, included, and accepted just as they are. She has a precarious perch of books on her nightstand, desk, and kitchen counter! Read about her journey and find activities for this book on her website, The Shaky Quaky Reading and Writing Gramma, https://kellydroberts.com/.

About the Illustrator

Jveria Gauhar is aspiring to be a Jane of All Trades. Eager to learn any new skill, she often jumps into projects feet first, with her head joining soon after. "Shaky Quaky Jake" is her debut illustrated book, which she has been extremely humbled and excited to share with the world. In addition to doodling, she is a black belt in Taekwondo. She is a professionally trained optometrist and has an eye for all things EYES! Jveria's most prized project, which has no end in sight, is being the mother to four creative kids and two uncreative cats!
She is based in Louisville, Kentucky.

Printed in the USA
CPSIA information can be obtained
at www.ICGtesting.com
CBHW041318010324
4848CB00052B/1262